T0193969

Evangelicals in a Frontier Town:

TUCSON, 1859-1918

First Edition

William A. Foltz;
Edited and with notes by Marilyn J. Martin

Order this book online at www.trafford.com
or email orders@trafford.com

Most Trafford titles are also available at major online book retailers.

Printed in the United States of America.

ISBN: 978-1-4669-2611-0 (sc)
ISBN: 978-1-4669-2612-7 (e)

Library of Congress Control Number: 2012912485

Trafford rev. 10/25/2012

www.trafford.com

North America & international
toll-free: 1 888 232 4444 (USA & Canada)
phone: 250 383 6864 • fax: 812 355 4082

contents

preface

THE PURPOSES OF THIS BOOK

This volume is intended:

- As a witness and a testimony to the positive things God has done for and through His people in Tucson, and what that means to us today.
- As a teaching and research tool. It includes guidelines for understanding spiritual principles, and for applying them to the contemporary scene. It is also to be a guide for further historical research. For these purposes there are discussion questions and practical exercises at the ends of the chapters.
- To describe some tragic mistakes of those who came before us, and to show how those mistakes continue to impact us.
- To show that by learning about and repenting of past mistakes, and reconciling with each other, God's people can not only recover much of what was lost, but gain new

ground. This will lead to revival and renewal in the Church, the in-gathering of the unconverted, and needed reform in society.

- To demonstrate the value of knowing our spiritual history as individuals, families, congregations, communities, and nations.
- To give readers tools and skills by which they can learn for themselves, and pass on their skills and learning to others.

The story presented in this volume is one we must not only learn ourselves, but learn to tell to others. It must be passed from generation to generation. And each generation must add its share to the story.

The Lord wants us to know what He has done, in history, through His people. That is the reason He gave His people a history book, the Bible. That is why we are to understand our own history.

Why does God want us to know this story?

- Because He wants us to know Him and His ways.
- Because He wants us to know His Church.
- Because He wants us to know His people.
- Because He wants us to know ourselves and our calling.
- Because He wants us to know our destiny and that of His Church.

It is hard to know where we are if we don't know how we got there, and from where. And if we don't know where we are, how will we know where we need to move on to?

It is my hope that this volume will be of service to both the evangelical and the secular historical community—and of course to those who have "dual citizenship" in those two communities.

This volume offers the evangelical community not only a look at its past, but Biblically based reasons why it should know and understand that past. This volume offers the secular historical community an introduction to an aspect of history to which it has paid little attention.

Tucson evangelicalism deserves "a place at the table" in the acknowledgment and study of the forces that have shaped and are shaping our community. Otherr things being equal, those seated at a table will learn more about each other, and come to appreciate each other more. May it be so in this case.

This volume is short. It is aimed at interested persons in both of the above-named communities. It combines qualities of popular and scholarly works. It does not purport to be a thorough or definitive treatment of its subject. It is a beginning. It is a seed from which, I hope, a seed will grow. It is, above all, a call to remembrance, of both the positive and the negative aspects of a people's past in our city. Without remembrance, there can be no learning. And without learning, there can be no growth or progress.

ROOTS AND WINGS

A tree with deep roots is stable. It can hold up under shifting ground and strong winds. A tree with shallow roots is not so. I was employed for some years in landscape maintenance. I often saw, and spend hours laboring over, fallen trees that had seemed strong and substantial, but had shallow roots.

Christians and Christian institutions are similar. They need to be deeply rooted and well grounded. Prayer, Bible study, fellowship with other Christians, and obedience to God's will are the primary means of becoming "deeply rooted." But there are secondary means as well. "Secondary" does not mean unimportant. There are many secondary means for becoming deeply rooted as a Chrristian. Christian education, Christian literature, and Christian entertainment and recreational facilities add much to the lives of believers.

Knowledge of our roots is a "secondary" means of becoming deeply rooted a Christians. It gives us depth and stability. It tells us how God has planted and nourished us. It gives us many clues as to what we should do today and in the future. That is, it gives us "wings" to fly in the direction in which God leads.

HISTORICAL RESEARCH

The subject matter of this volume is potentially of interest both to Tucson's evangelical Christian community and to the secular historical community. That is not to say that it should be of equal interest to the two communities, or that it should be of interest for all of the same reasons. But as pure history, it should be of interest to both. Several secular historians in Tucson and elsewhere have encouraged me in my work, and expressed interest in my findings.

This work is, in some ways, a continuation of the work of past historians and compilers of information, such as Estelle Lutrell, long-time librarian at the University of Arizona. Writers like C. L. Sonnichsen, who wrote a book on Tucson, show a detailed knowledge of evangelical causes and personalities. I wish I had learned this years earlier. In the case of Dr. Sonnichsen, that might have made it possible for me to ask his help and advice on this project.

THE PROBLEMS

AMERICANS' NEGLECT OF HISTORY

Several explanations have been offered as to why Americans in general, and American evangelicals in particular, are not too interested in history. Later we will deal with a particular problem in Tucson and the West. Otherwise, we will not discuss them at length. But here is something to think about. Suppose your "significant other" was reminiscing to you about things that had happened in his or her life before you met. Suppose you were to cut this person off midsentence and say, "I don't want to hear about what happened to you before I met you. Al that matters is what you have experienced with me!

What kind of response to you think that would provoke? What would it do to your relationship with that person? If a Christian shows no interest in what God has done in the past, isn't he or she basically saying the same thing to the Lord? (This scenario is probably an even better illustration of what it says about the message we're sending God if we have no interest in Bible study.)

If history is unimportant, why did God give His people a history book, the Bible? And if what He did for and through His people then is important, isn't what He has done since also important?

It should become more and more clear as this volume progresses that our past, our history, does matter. And that God uses it to speak to us.

WHY WE SHOULD STUDY OUR HISTORY

THE "I'M FROM . . ." SYNDROME

In Tucson, and many other places in the West, most of the population, especially the Anglo population, is nonindigenous. Some of the younger people may have been born here, but most have little understanding of what makes Tucson distinctive. When many Tucsonans talk about their backgrounds, we hear them say, "I'm from . . ." as they launch into personal histories that have little to do with Tucson.

The same is really true of many churches. They reflect mindsets and styles of worship that were developed in other places, often in other eras. Even most "contemporary" worship services could just as easily have been experienced in New York or Chicago in the 1970s or in Tucson in 2000. Even Hispanics—and, to a lesser degree, Native Americans—are being caught up in this homogenization.

In longer-settled regions, things are different. On the Eastern seaboard, members of some congregations can go to the church cemeteries and visit the graves of ancestors who worshiped there two hundred or more years ago. That is an extreme example. But it does make a real difference if our grandparents or great-grandparents worshiped in the same church, or even the same city, as we do. It makes us feel part of the past.

THE NEED FOR ACCURATE INFORMATION

I have become the unwitting originator of a bit of what might charitably be called evangelical "folklore." It surrounds D. L. Moody's 1899 Tucson campaign, which is described in chapter 6. More accurate terms might be "rumors" and "distortions." I have heard things said one on one or in small group discussions, and sometimes from pulpits and podiums, that certainly don't correspond to the facts as other people and I have discovered them.

My favorite rumor is that the Tucson City Council responded to Moody and his group thus: they "ran them out of town." If any reader has documentary evidence of that, please present it!

This volume will be a corrective to that problem. If a false report is given, the prson who is unsure of the truth can refer to this volume for the facts.

SOLUTIONS

We seek knowledge of that which we consider important. We consider important that which we think will help us live our lives or do our work. The main reason most Americans—evangelical and otherwise—have so little interest in history is that they don't hink is will help them do those things.

In recent years, two movements have come to the fore in evangelicalism that present us with an urgent need to study and understand history. They are spiritual mapping and representative reconciliation.

Spiritual mapping can be defined as studying the historical, social, political, and spiritual history and present realities of a community in order to understand and minister to the needs of that community. A good introduction to this movement is John Dawson's Taking Our Cities for God: How to Break Spiritual Strongholds (Creation House, 1989).

Representative reconciliation can be defined as a process by which persons speaking on behalf of the communities they represent seek peace through reconciliation. An introduction to this movement is John Dawson's Healing America's Wounds (Regal Books, 1994). Dawson makes many references to the frontier West. A whole chapter (chapter 12, pp. 145-60) deals with the 1864 Sand Creek (Colorado) Massacre. It was an event similar to what took place at Camp Grant near Tucson, but even more inexcusable.

WHAT YOU CAN DO

There are several practical, spiritual things the reader of this book can do in response to it:

- Pray. The Spirit of God will lead you into all truth. Don't rely on the insights I present here. Only the Lord can tell you exactly what to believe about what you read here, and what to do about it.
- Read. And read carefully. If you read hastily or superficially, you may miss something important. It may be that parts of this volume have no direct application to your situation. But to know which do and which do not, you will need to read the entire volume carefully.

- Apply and Ask Questions. Sometimes we make the mistake of grasping at answers before we have asked the right questions. There can be no valid answers without valid questions. There are questions for discussion and topics for further research at the ends of most chapters. And feel free to develop and pursue answers to your own questions.
- Minister. The main reason Christians need to know the history of their city is so that they can better understand how to minister there. Of what use is the knowledge to be gained from this volume if it doesn't help our people grow, in both knowledge and Christlike ministry?

format and source attribution

The format of this book has been designed to be as accessible as possible. It has also been designed to make the book interactive. Its purpose is to engage the emotions and will, as well as the intellect.

Source attribution is a bit more casual in this volume than in a scholarly work. Where feasible, it is included in the body of the text. Where that would break the continuity, it is given at the end of the chapter.

The Special Collections section of the University of Arizona Library has played a pivotal role in the research on this topic. It has been far and away my most useful and versatile source. Unlike the Main Library, it still uses a simple file-card catalog system.

terminology

EVANGELICAL

In this volume, this term is used in a broader sense than it is sometimes used today. Rick Leis, a Tucson pastor, defines basic evangelicalism as follows: "Evangelicals teach salvation through faith in Christ, and they reject the efficacy of the sacraments and good works alone." This broader definition is the one I have used in this volume.

By contrast, the narrower definition of this term, sometimes referred to as "big E" evangelicalism, adds such doctrines as Biblical inerrancy, and even positions on Church polity and social issues, to the equation.

Even a cursory reading of the literature of the time demonstrates that the Protestant churches of a hundred and more years ago were more united around the broader definition of evangelicalism than they have been since. Due allowance must be made for sharp differences of opinion in some denominations on issues such as the sacraments. These differences were especially notable in the Episcopal Church. But in general, there churches were able to support and promote basic evangelical beliefs.

IDENTIFICATIONAL REPENTANCE AND REPRESENTATIVE RECONCILIATION

"When we identify with the sins of our people and ask forgiveness of God and those who have been sinned against . . . . We identify and represent those who committed the sins, and beg forgiveness from the people who represent the families and groups that were sinned against. As representatives, we express our deep sorrow, commit to a godly direction, and ask for forgiveness."

introduction (2012)

The purposes of this volume are (1) To inform the community about the background and history of Tucson's evangelicals, (2) to encourage people to think about how that history relates to our time and to today's needs, and (3) to encourage and stimulate firther research on this subject.

The research was done from the early 1970s through the late 1990s. Since then, there have been two major developments: The Internet revolution in the retrieval and dissemination of information, and my relocation (in 2007) to West Columbia, SC.

Many documents that were formerly hard to come by can now be read and downloaded online. The most notable example—which I heartily recommend to the reader—is the book, ROCHESTER FORD:THE STORY OF A SUCCESSFUL CHRISTIAN LAWYER, BY HIS FATHER AND MOTHER, SAMUEL H. FORD AND SALLIE ROCHESTER FORD (Saint Louis: M. P. Moody, 1904.) It gives a much more thorough overview of the Tucson of circa 1900 than is possible in my volume.

The fact that I now reside 1,600 air miles from Tucson makes it all the more urgent that other researchers investigate this topic. As the incompleteness of Chapter Eight will indicate, there is a crying need for further research on evangelical beginnings among the various ethnic minorities.

Space does not permit a recognition of all of the family and friends who have aided in the preparation of this volume. Let me mention my editor, Marilyn Martin, without whom this project would never have seen daylight. I also thank the staffs of the Arizona Historical Society Library, and of Special Collections, University of Arizoan Library.

chapter 1

A WITNESS AND A TESTIMONY

Why Should We Study Our History?

It has been pointed out that we Americans have difficulty understanding and dealing with our own history. A congregation or ministry may (or may not) be interested in its own history, perhaps even in that of its parent denomination or group. But church history in general is not perceived by the average evangelical as relevant to what God has called him to do.

No one denies the importance of that question of relevance. Why should the Church of Jesus Christ concern itself with this matter? Where is the Biblical sanction for such concern?

A BIBLICAL PERSPECTIVE

The Bible was written long before the advent of scientific historiography. One would therefore not expect to find in it a lengthy discourse on the importance of historical studies.

But I see an even more important reason why the subject is not dealt with: It never occurred to the people of the Bible to regard their history as unimportant or irrelevant. That it might have been seen that way they would have regarded as nonsense.

The word <u>remember</u> appears in the Bible about 140 times, mostly in the Old Testament. It us used in a variety of ways. In some instances, as is Psalm 77:11, it refers to events of the distant past.

Often the call to remembrance takes the form of a simple declarative statement. For example: "I am the Lord your God, who brought you out of Egypt, out of the house of slavery" (Deut. 5:6, NIV).

PARALLELS TO PERSONAL WITNESS AND TESTIMONY

A. An individual tells others about (witnesses to) the history of what has done in his life. This is his testimony of that history.
B. This spreads that witness and testimony beyond the individual's place, and people remember the testimony beyond the time frame in which it was stated.
C. People are blessed who were not there to experience the exact things the witness experienced.

GOD HAS PRESERVED BOTH LIVING AND RECORDED WITNESSES SO THAT WE, HIS PEOPLE, MAY BE BLESSED AND INSTRUCTED BY EVENTS WE DID NOT PERSONALLY EXPERIENCE AND IN WHICH WE DID NOT PARTICIPATE.

JUST AS AN INDIVIDUAL HAS A TESTIMONY, SO DOES A FAMILY, A CONGREGATION, OR THE CHURCH IN A COMMUNITY, STATE, OR NATION.

EXERCISES

1. If you have not already done so, prepare a written personal testimony. Include something about your family background, your early religious training and experiences, and what drew you to Christ.
2. Write a spiritual history of your family. Begin with the earliest ancestor(s) you know who did something of spiritual significance. For example, did any of your forebears immigrate to America to escape religious persecution? Were any in full-time Christian service or prominent laypersons?

chapter 2

PRINCIPLES THAT STAND THE TEST OF TIME

THE GREAT COMMISSION

Matt. 28:19-20: "All authority in heaven and on earth has been given to me. Therefore go and make disciples of all nations, baptizing them . . . and teaching them to obey everything I have commanded you . . . ."

This statement has been universally recognized by the Church as Jesus's "marching orders" to spread his Gospel as widely as possible. Whom he was addressing has been a point of controversy in the Church.

This volume takes the viewpoint that Christ was addressing himself to all Christians, clergy and laity, throughout all of history. This reflects the belief of most modern evangelicals.

According to this viewpoint, the responsibility of leaders and led, vocational Christian workers and laypersons, may differ in degree, but not in kind.

We will examine how Tucson's early evangelicals understood their Great Commission responsibilities and how they sought to fulfill them.

CHRISTIAN UNITY

It is taken for granted that unity and harmony among Christians is a New Testament mandate (John 17:20-23). But again, exactly who and what are involved in that unity are points of controversy.

I see no clear and simple solutions to this controversy. Given all the beliefs affirmed—and all the beliefs rejected—by different people who call themselves Christians, it is sometimes hard to know whether to call someone brother or heretic.

A major tension throughout Tucson history has been between unity and division. It has also been a major theme in Church history. In general, the period between c. 1870 and c1918 witnessed in Tucson a movement from unity to disunity. This was true both in the secular and in the religious realm. We will examine this disunity and ask what heritage it has left us and what we should do about it.

Identificational repentance is defined by missiologist C. Peter Wagner as "When we identify with the sins of our people and ask forgiveness of God and those who have been sinned against."[1]

Rick Leis, a Tucson pastor, adds: "We do this as representatives of the ones who actually committed the sin against another people group. We identify and represent those who committed the sins, and beg forgiveness from the people that represent the families and groups . . . sinned against. As representatives, we express our deep sorrow, and commit to a godly direction and ask forgiveness."[2]

In 1871 a terrible event occurred. It originated in Tucson. It is now known as the Camp Grant Massacre. It will be referred to several times throughout this work. A few years ago, a "reconciliation" was held in connection with that tragedy. It well illustrates this principle.

Representative reconciliation completes the process begun by identificational repentance. It typically involves a long period of interaction between the groups of people concerned. The process often leads to a public ceremony called a "reconciliation." At a reconciliation, representatives of the offending group briefly confess the offense, express repentance on behalf of their group, and as an act of restitution plege to relate to the offended group in friendship, justice, and helpfulness. The offended group(s), in turn accept the repentance and other overtures and likewise pledge to relate to the offenders in friendship. If they consider it appropriate, they might also confess some wrongs on behalf of their own people. But this is not the norm. An example will be given later.

THE TOOL: SPIRITUAL MAPPING

An important tool to use in this task is called spiritual mapping. This is the study of a community in order to discern its spiritual condition and to meet its spiritual needs.

Spiritual mapping combines spiritual and scholarly disciplines. It joins religious to secular subject matter. The information it compiles and the issues it deals with are often of interest to believers and nonbelievers alike.

Origins and beginnings are of particular importance. Why was a community (or a school, a church, or a business) founded? Who were the founds? What were their vision and their dreams?

Another key issues is this: What kinds of wounds have the community sustained? Has there been military or civil violence? Class or racial conflict? What kinds of pain, resentment, or fear remain from these would from the past?

The purpose of answering these questions is twofold: First, to give credit where credit is due to those who have gone before us and prepared the path on which we walk. Second, and even more important, to diagnose the problems that need to be dealt with and the wounds that need to be healed. This is so that those problems can be acknowledged and dealt with and so that people can be reconciled to each other.

A prominent theme in this volume is the interaction between different groups of people. Specifically, the theme is unity versus division.

Historically, Tucson's elite have liked to think of our city and portray it as a place of racial, ethnic, class, and religious tolerance and harmony. But how true was that in the past? And how true is it now?

If there has been such unity, on what has it been based? How deep or superficial has it been? Who has been included or excluded?

I will ask—and encourage the reader to ask—questions like these: How significant is it that Tucson began as a walled fortress inside which diverse groups bonded together as allies for protection against a common enemy? Was that a phenomenon that passes with the tearning down of the presidio walls, or did those walls represent a mindset that persisted? What kind of "walls," [jusical or psychological, have been built and/or demolished since? Who have been the "alies" and who the "enemy"?

The most important question is this? How has all this affected the evangelical community and its witness? If it has disrupted that witness, could that have been prevented? More important, how much of the damage can be undone, and how? And most important of all, how can we avoid the traps our forebears fell into?

A very delicate matter here is how to describe the relationship of Jewish pioneers to the evangelical community and the contribution of these Jewish pioneers to the life of Tucson without sounding awkward or patronizing.

In this connection, it is important to ask, Can a spiritual principle be applied by anyone, or only by an informed evangelical? In this volume I assume that anyone can apply such a principle who properly understands it. Many examples could be cited. One is the use of the Mosaic Law as the basis for the legal codes of many Western nations.

NOTES TO CHAPTER 2

1 George Otis, The Last of the Giants, 84-102.
2 Rick Leis to author, Sept. 29, 1997.

chapter 3

EARLY TUCSON CHURCH LIFE

TUCSON'S FIRST CHRISTIANS

Tucson's first Christians arrived about a hundred years before there was a place officially called Tucson. (The Tohono O'odham nation of Native Americans who inhabited the area called it Schoohson, which means "black base" or "at the foot of the black mountain." The mountain to which they referred was either that now called Sentinel Peak, on what was later called "A" Mountain, or nearby Tumamoc Hill.)

Along with or closely following the Spanish conquistadores who came into the New World came the padres, missionaries for Roman Catholic Christianity. The most notable in our area was Eusebio Franciso Kino, an Italian Jesuit who labored in the region from 1687 until 1711. He was a man of many talents—as a peacemaker, rancher, miner, explorer,[1] and historian. The missions he founded in the Arizona-Sonora desert became the economic foundations of those later established in California.

In 1775-76, an expedition left Culiacán, Mexico. It was led by Colonel Juan Bautista de Anza the younger. Its original purpose was to found a colony on the site of San Francisco. In the process the presidio of San Augustin del Tucson was founded.

Despite ups and downs, the relationship among Hispanics, Natives, and the Catholic Church has endured for centuries. When evangelicals arrived, they encountered a well-established organization that considered itself well able to meet the spiritual needs of any and all Arizonans. Neither the Catholics nor the evangelicals understood or approved of one another. Neither group really acknowledged the spiritual legitimacy of the other. In the years since the frontier period, that mutual perception has modified some. But the process of change is a slow one.

EARLY EVANGELICAL LIFE: AN OVERVIEW

Most of the Anglos who settled in Tucson in the fifteen years after the Gadsden Purchase of 1854 were of Protestant backgrounds. Some no doubt were evangelicals. But until about 1870, the Protestant community remained unorganized and passive.

Several factors contributed to this. For one thing, the Anglo community consisted mostly of young unmarried males. When they did marry, it was nearly always to Mexican women who were Catholic. Their children were invariable raised in the Catholic faith of the mothers, and some of the fathers eventually converted to it. The private lives of many of the men were marred by the vices that were so readily catered to in frontier Tucson. Besides, the denominational backgrounds of the church-minded were too diverse to make formation of congregations easy.

Around 1870 all this started to change. Protestant preachers began to visit Tucson, holding services and otherwise ministering. Without regular church buildings, they were very creative in the settings and subject matters of their preaching. Catholic Bishop John Baptist Salpointe and his assistant and successor, Peter Bourgarde, complained to their superiors that the Protestants "preach anywhere on all subjects, sometimes in the streets an sometimes in the gambling halls."[2]

Between 1871 and 1881, four tiny Protestant congregations were formed: in 1876 a Union Church, which later branched off into Trinity Presbyterian; in 1879 what is now First Methodist; and in 1881 Grace Episcopal and what is now First Baptist.

Rev. Jackson, Superintendent of Presbyterian Missions for the Territories, received the following petition from Tucson in April 1876: "In order to secure Protestant Church privileges for Tucson, we the undersigned members . . . in the various Evangelical Churches, do hereby request . . . to organize into a Presbyterian Church, and secure for us a good and efficient minister." Five petitioners authorized Jackson to transfer their letters of church membership from out of town. An additional twenty-three, including territorial Governor Safford and Star editor L. C. Hughes, pledged "our hearty cooperation and support."[3]

Later that month, Jackson conducted worship services at the Pima Country Courthouse, while the "whole Protestant . . . community" was giving the movement "their hearty sympathy." the church building was completed in 1879 in the Court House Plaza under the supervision of Sam Hughes.

DIFFICULTIES FOR THE PROTESTANT CHURCHES

Several factors made life difficult for these churches.

THE MAJORITY STATUS OF CATHOLICISM

In 1890, the U.S. Census put the population of Pima County, of which Tucson is the county seat, at 6,780. The four Protestant churches had a total communicant membership of 235.[3]

The Catholic bishops, priests, and religious who ministered in frontier Arizona were nearly all European immigrants, mostly from France. Many were persons of great education and ability. They made a deep impression on Catholic and non-Catholic alike. They established Tucson's first hospitals and schools.

As long as the Protestant community kept quiet, the Catholic Church got along well with it. But as it became more activist, the Catholics came to view it as a threat. And since they regarded governmental agencies as agents of Protestant ideas, they also came into conflict with them. They opposed "sects" and the government with all the considerable skill and resources at their command.[4]

LACK OF INTEREST ON THE PART OF THE MALE POPULATION

In the late nineteenth century, Protestant church membership in the United States was about two-thirds female. That state of affairs was well reflected in Tucson.

The leading men of frontier communities regarded churches as essential to a stable, civilized community life. When a congregation began, they would actively promote the effort, contribute to the building fund, and often sign on as charter members. But once the church was on its feet, they often showed little further interest. Others, like famed diarist George O. Hand, made the rounds of services at all churches, without joining one.[5]

The fraternal lodges, especially the Freemasons, were enjoying a heyday nationwide. Most non-Catholic men of any prominence belonged to one or more. They tended to promote a universalistic, works-oriented religiosity.

Few leading men (clergy excepted) actively championed the evangelical cause. One was attorney Rochester Ford (see chapter 4).

ECONOMIC DIFFICULTIES

Tucson's economy was in a depressed state for most of the frontier period. The boom that started when the railroad reached Tucson in 1880 didn't last. Conditions became so bad that Tucson's population fell from 7,000 in 1880 to 5,000 in 1890. Most of the leading businesses were ruined, unable to compete with cheaper goods brought in by railroad. Their owners, men who had led Tucson in the 1860s and 1870s, spent their last years in relative—and sometimes abject—poverty. The panic of 1893 and a terrible drought complicated matters.[6]

Also during the 1890s, Tucson lost its leadership in Arizona affairs to Phoenix and Maricopa County. It has never regained that leadership. Nor has it ever stopped resenting Maricopa County's dominance.

These troubles made for a highly mobile middle- and working-class population. They also kept missionary activities, both Catholic and Protestant, dependent on financial support from the East. Both factors retarded the development of local lay leadership.

THE DIFFICULTY OF ATTRACTING AND KEEPING PASTORS

Few Protestant pastors wanted to labor in such a remote and difficult field. Those who did often came for health reasons. Most of the churches buried one or two pastors during the period. It could take a long time to find a replacement pastor. First Baptist Church was without a pastor from 1890 to 1895. At one point it had only twenty members and was not holding regular services.[7]

THE ECONOMIC AND POLITICAL POWER OF THE VICE INDUSTRY

An article that appeared in the Arizona Weekly Star in 1881 reported that forty-one places on Meyer Street alone sold intoxicating beverages. Saloons, gambling halls, and houses of prostitution operated around the clock. Gambling was outlawed in 1906, and Arizona "went dry" in 1914. But prostitution was legal until 1926!

Top gamblers and saloon keepers played a leading role in Tucson politics and other community affairs. Some earned reputations as gentlemen and benefactors of the needy. They were formidable opponents.

THE SLOW, STEADY GROWTH OF THE EVANGELICAL COMMUNITY

The evangelical community in Tucson enjoyed some advantages:

- There was a social activism that appealed to many. Prohibition, civic reform, missions to minority groups, and medical work were eventually included.
- There were several outstanding personalities who were respected by the community and were willing and able to influence it.
- There were effective Protestant women's organizations. These included denominational and congregational societies and parachurch organizations such as the Women's Christian Temperance Union. They were the most effective Christian disciple-building mechanisms in America and were among the country's most effective grassroots organizations. The most outstanding figure in these groups in Tucson was Josephine B. Hughes. In fact if not in name, she was co-editor, with her husband Louis C. Hughes, of the Arizona Daily Star. More about her will appear in chapter 4.

Slow progress was made. By the 1890s, missionary work had been started among Mexicans, Papagos, and Chinese. The Salvation Army began its Tucson ministry in 1893. In 1900, the black community organized its first congregation, Second Baptist Church, later renamed Mt. Calvary Baptist Church.

The religious revival that had begun in Wales in 1904 quickly spread throughout the world. Everywhere, including Tucson, there was a heightened interest in evangelism and missions. The

1906 U.S. Census showed about a 150 percent increase in Protestant church membership since 1890. The difficult frontier period was over.

Despite the broad but shallow popular Christianity of the day, there was open hostility to the Christian faith in some circles. Magdalene Windes, whose husband, Romulus A. Windes, founded the Lone Star Baptist Church in Prescott, wrote of several incidents in that town:

A prominent man . . . a merchant, kept The Mistakes of Moses (by Robert Ingersoll) lying on his counter He showed it to me with the remark that it was a better book than the Bible.

One day a man accosted my husband on the street with the inquiry, "Well, sir, how is Jesus Christ today?" Another man openly stated that in his opinion Jesus Christ was an illegitimate child . . . .

One sabbath, when we entered our house of worship, we found that someone had broken in and tried to wreck our organ . . . . Judge (Henry W.) Fleury called it the work of a crazy iconoclast. It seemed to me just plain spite.

A man came to our house one night . . . . The man . . . had threatened to cut the heart out of my husband because he had baptized his wife while he was away from home . . . .

Another man, whose misconduct had resulted in his being excluded from the church, waylaid Mr. Windes . . . and threatened him with violence . . . . [8]

The Methodists, from the start, dreamed great dreams. The Arizona Mission was formally organized in 1881. Almost immediately, there was a proposal for an Arizona Wesleyan University. It never came to be, but the fact that it was proposed is significant.[9]

Some outstanding Methodist men came to Arizona to help build those dreams. M. M. Bovard, Arizona District Superintendent from 1890 to 1896, later became the first president of the University of Southern California. The first pastor of Tucson's Methodist church, Joseph F. Perry, was a later made a bishop.[10]

QUESTIONS FOR DISCUSSION

1. What difference, if any, would it have made in the establishment of Protestant Christianity in Tucson if there had not be a strong Catholic presence?
2. If you had been a church leader in frontier Tucson, what steps would you have taken to promote evangelism and church planting? In particular, what would you have done to reach the male population?

SUGGESTIONS FOR FURTHER RESEARCH

1. Most of what we know of early Tucson evangelicalism comes to us from a few personalities in whom church or secular historians have taken an interest. Most of this interest is due to their positions in society or their relative wealth. What about that "silent majority" of believers who quietly keep churches and ministries going? It would be helpful to have letters, reminiscences, or records from the hands of middle- and working-class believers of this period.
2. Another "silent majority" were the women. (After all, most of the early evangelicals were women. In fact, it was only after a sizeable number of Anglo women had arrived in

Tucson that a viable evangelical community became possible.) I have read many names in church and newspaper records. But the only evangelical woman of whose activities I have found an extensive record was Josephine B. Hughes.

NOTES TO CHAPTER 3

1 It was Kino who discovered that California is part of North America and not an island as had been thought.

2 Abigail A. Van Slyck, "What the Bishop learned: The Importance of Claiming Space at Tucson's Church Plaza," Journal of Arizona History, Summer 1998, 121-40.

3 Leland H. Scott, Twelve Decades . . . and Beyond: Glimpses into the History of Methodism's "First Church" in Tucson, Arizona (Tucson: _____________, 1999).

4

5

6

7

8 "The Devil Kept His Cauldron Boiling: The Reminiscences of Magdalene Ann Windes, Wife of Arizona's First Baptist Missionary," ed. Mona Lange McCroskey, Journal of Arizona History, Autumn 1998, 244-47.

9 Chilton C. McPheeters, Enclyclopedia of World Methodism (___________: United Methodist Publishing House, 1974), 2373-74.

10 Ibid.

chapter 4

TWO OUTSTANDING LAYPERSONS

Josephine B. Hughes and Rochester Ford

JOSEPHINE HUGHES

Josephine Brawley Hughes (1839-1926) was married to Louis C. (L. C.) Hughes (1842-1915). Both were from Pennsylvania, both graduates of Alleghany College. Both believed in and upheld Christian values. But Josephine was the more evangelical in her theology. And she probably did more to promote evangelical church life and evangelical social ethics than any other person in Tucson church history.

L. C.'s brother Sam had settled in Tucson in the 1850s. He had become a successful merchant and beloved community leader. L. C., an attorney, followed Sam in 1871. Josephine, a teacher, could not join him at first. But later that year she traveled to San Diego, California. In 1872, she made the five hundred-mile trip to Tucson by stagecoach. It took five days and nights. Most of the time she had an infant daughter on her lap and a rifle in her hand. In one place, the Apaches missed them by just twenty-four hours.[1]

Josephine arrived in a Tucson where "girls didn't go to school. There wasn't a Protestant church or a daily newspaper. Floors were all made of dirt."[2]

For several years, there had been a movement to start a public school in Tucson. Shortly after Josephine arrived, Apache raids intensified to the point that it was thought inadvisable to send female teachers to Arizona. So in 1873 Josephine became the first public school teacher in Arizona. When it was safe for other teachers to come, she gave up that responsibility.

In 1877, L. C. and Josephine founded the Arizona Weekly Star, which later became the Arizona Daily Star. It was the great labor of their lives. L. C. was editor in chief. Josephine was assistant editor—at least in name. In fact, she was co-editor. The couple ran the paper for thirty years.

The Star was a fighting newspaper. That was not unusual on the frontier. What was unusual was what the editors fought for: women's suffrage, prohibition, the closing of gambling halls and houses of prostitution, Sunday closure of businesses, and prison reform.

Back then, newspaper editing was a rough and sometimes dangerous occupation. In 1979, a gang of thugs burst into the Star office. They broke L. C.'s arm in the presence of Josephine and other Star employees and smashed the printing press. During L. C.'s term as territorial governor (1893-95), he was once assaulted on the street in Phoenix by a local newspaper reporter. How influential were L. C.'s enemies in Phoenix? His assailant got off with a five-dollar fine!

The Star's editorial page, along with feminist and anti-saloon statements, had numerous Bible quotes, and a column that appeared twice a week consisted mainly of Bible verses, especially from Proverbs.

Josephine's individual contributions to Tucson were even more impressive than those she made with her husband. She was head of both the Women's Suffrage ________________ and the Women's Christian Temperance Union. She encouraged such leaders as Frances Willard. When the movement to start Tucson's first Protestant church began, Josephine was also a leader in that effort (see chapter 4). And she was called "The Mother of Methodism in Arizona."

An 1894 incident that involved Josephine and her son, John T. Hughes, says a great deal about those times—and about how times have changed. Josephine and her son, then twenty, attended the National Suffrage Convention in Washington, D.C. Susan B. Anthony recognized them. The woman John had been brought up to call Aunt Susan "captured and took him to the platform." She delivered a glowing tribute to his parents and him. Then, in a little ceremony that included a laying on of hands, she dubbed him "The Suffrage Knight of Arizona."[3]

John lived up to that title. As a state representative in Arizona's first State Legislature in 1912, he introduced an amendment to the Arizona Constitution on women's suffrage. It went to the voters as an initiative. The all-male electorate voted overwhelmingly to open the franchise to Arizona's women. This was seven years before the Nineteenth Amendment to the U.S. Constitution was adopted!

The later years of Josephine and L. C. were difficult. Several business ventures failed. They lost the Star in 1907. L. C. died in 1915, followed by John in 1921. Illnesses, accidents, and financial distress forced Josephine to spend her last years with her daughter in California. She died there in 1926.

Josephine lived to see most of the reforms she and L. C. had advocated written into the laws of the United States, Arizona, or Tucson. In her last years, Josephine received several honors from official Arizona. Shortly after her death, a plaque was placed in the rotunda of the State Capitol in Phoenix. It referred to her as "The Mother of Arizona."

ROCHESTER FORD

> We know that in everything God works for good with those who love him, who are called according to his purpose.
>
> —Romans 8:28, RSV

A tragic aspect of life in Tucson for well over a hundred years has been the steady influx of "health refugees" (of whom the author of this book is one). They have made an invaluable contribution to the life of our community. But that community has been forced to witness their suffering, and in many cases their deaths. Rochester Ford was a classic example.

Ford was born about 1860 in Saint Louis. He was the son of Samuel H. Ford, a Baptist minister and magazine editor, and Sallie Rochester Ford, a well-known Christian novelist.[4] Admitted to the bar in 1883, he soon built up a lucrative law practice in Saint Louis. He also spent several years on the law school faculty of that city's Washington University.[5] Ford was a man of faith, and at age twenty-six he was elected vice moderator of the Missouri Baptist Convention.[6]

No one knows how far Ford might have gone in one of America's leading cities had he remained there. But a health problem, probably asthma, made that impossible. Since 1885, he had been representing Southern Arizona clients. (One land case with which he was involved, Colin Cameron vs. the United States, remained in the courts for thirty-four years, until 1911!)[8]

After two lengthy stays at Arizona health resorts, he settled permanently in Tucson in 1890 or 1891.

Ford made such an impression on the leading people of Tucson that when he had been a resident just two years he was made chancellor of the young University of Arizona. He also served two years as city attorney. An active and progressive Democrat, he was legal counsel for the Citizen's Good Government Club.[9]

Ford was no less a success socially. He was a leading member of the Owl's Club, whose membership then essentially consisted of the residents of an upscale boarding house for socially prominent, morally respectable bachelors (Ford never married).[10] Tucson native Bill Freyse later immortalized the Owl's Club in his nationally syndicated comic strip "Our Boarding House with Major Hoople."

The Tucson Citizen described Ford this way: "Of commanding presence, he possessed a charm of manner and a degree of personal magnetism which . . . fitted him to shine in any circle . . . ."[11]

Ford served as a deacon and was Sunday School superintendent at First Baptist Church. When the church was without a pastor from 1890 to 1895, he sometimes preached. He paid for the renovation of the building's interior. Without his support, the congregation almost certainly would have folded during the difficult time without a pastor. Ford also made financial contributions to other churches and ministries in Tucson. He greatly aided D. L. Moody's Tucson campaign of 1899 (discussed in chapter 6).

In view of his fervent evangelicalism and his Southern roots (his parents had been ardent Confederate sympathizers), some would find it strange that Ford both endorsed and practiced the ethnic and religious tolerance and fraternization for which Tucson was once known. He spoke well of the Mexican-American community in an article he wrote for the September 1902 issue of Out West Magazine, which was reprinted as a promotional brochure by the Tucson Chamber of Commerce. (This article will be quoted in chapter 9.) Selim Franklin and Leo Goldschmidt, the two business associates and fellow Owl's Club members who provided future generations of secular Tucsonans with most of their knowledge of Ford, were both Jews.

Rochester Ford's health steadily worsened after the turn of the century. He died on August 14, 1903. It is obvious from the tone of the written tributes that followed that his death had been expected. There are none of the expressions of shock that usually accompany a sudden, premature death.

But the tributes could hardly have been warmer. An editorial that appear in the Arizona Daily Star on August 16, 1903, read: "He was always the exemplary gentleman reflecting a good light, pure, moral, and religious influences . . . . The deceased was a striking example of the good fruits which come from early Christian training."

Both of Ford's parents survived him. In 1904, they published a biography, Rochester Ford: The Story of a Successful Christian Lawyer, by His Father and Mother (Saint Louis: M. P. Moody, 1904). The only extant copies of which I know are housed in special collections in Missouri and Alabama. A number of Southern Baptist historians have read the book. One of the described it to me as "not very informative."

Sallie Ford, in particular, was affected by the death of her only child (Samuel Ford, previously married, had other children). In 1906, she came to Tucson and visited First Baptist Church. The church was then in the midst of constructing a new building, and she intended to make a large donation. Sallie Ford proposed that the church be renamed after her son. According to the minutes of the meeting that dealt with her proposal, it was voted down only after a long and emotional debate. Some friends who were members of First Baptist Church at the time tell me that they are clad the did not have to grow up in the Rochester Ford Memorial Baptist Church. This is especially true of those who grew up while The Jack Benny Show was still on the air. Even though Sallie Ford's proposal was turned down, she made the donation she had intended to make.

Romans 8:28 has operated around Rochester Ford's life for over one hundred years. Who knows how many thousands of people have benefited from his efforts? Few of them will ever hear his name. But as poet Vachel Linsay wrote in "John Peter Altgeld," "It is far, far better to live in the people than in a name."

QUESTIONS FOR DISCUSSION

1. What other couples have you read or heard of, or known personally, who aided and complemented each other's careers and ministries as did Josephine and L. C. Hughes? If you knew the couple, what impact did they have on your own life?
2. The difference in the relationship that existed between Christian women and feminism one hundred years ago and that today is startling. What do you think caused the rift? Can it ever be healed? If so, how?
3. How much difference can one person really make? How much difference can you yourself make?
4. Does a story like that of Rochester Ford say anything to us about the health problems or seemingly premature deaths of people we have known? Is so, what?
5. What does the story of Ford say about "the good of one versus the good of many"?

SUGGESTIONS FOR FURTHER RESEARCH

1. Study or write about a couple who have had an impact on history in your own lifetime.
2. Why on earth has no one ever written a book about L. C. and Josephine Hughes? Might you be the one to do it?
3. Do you think there are other early Tucson evangelicals whose contributions have been all but forgotten? Would it be best to allow them to be remembered and rewarded by God alone? Or would it be profitable for researchers to invest time and effort in learning about them? Might you be the one to do it?

NOTES TO CHAPTER 4

[1] George H. Kelly, Arizona Daily Star, June 14, 1925.

[2] Laura Stone, Arizona Daily Star, March 12, 1982.

[3] George H. Kelly, Arizona Daily Star, June 14, 1925.

[4] Several of her novels are on microfilm in the Special Collections Department of the University of Arizona Library in Tucson.

[5] A 75th Anniversary History of the First Baptist church, Tucson, Arizona (Tucson, 1956). UA Special Collections.

[6] Rochester Ford File, Selim Franklin Papers. This file contains literally hundreds of letters, mostly business letters, written by Ford to Franklin between 1885 and 1903. UA Special Collections.

[7] See the Rochester Ford biographical file, especially a 1933 letter from Leo Goldschmidt to Estelle Luttrell. UA Special Collections.

[8] Rochester Ford File.

[9] 75th Anniversary History, Rochester Ford biographical file.

[10] Rochester Ford biographical file.

[11] "Rochester Ford," editorial in the Tucson Citizen, August 17, 1903, 3.

chapter 5
AN INTERLUDE

A Biblical Principle in the Founding of the University of Arizona

This chapter is called an interlude because it represents a departure from the pattern of the other chapters. Most of the other events described in this book had an overtly Christian character. And most of the major players introduced elsewhere were active evangelicals. In this chapter I a thoroughly secular event involving, for the most part, thoroughly secular personalities, is interpreted from an evangelical perspective.

In frontier society, a man could go to the top very quickly. In Tucson, attorney Selim M. Franklin certainly did. In 1884 Franklin, twenty-five years old and a resident of Tucson for one year, was elected to the Territorial Legislature as a Democrat. That made him part of the wild, tarnished, but very productive Thirteenth Legislature.

Franklin was to play a key role in bringing the University of Arizona to Tucson. In a 1922 address to the university community, he described what happened. This chapter has been based on a typescript of that address.[1]

Everyone knew that huge prizes would be up for grabs in the 1885 session. As usual, there would be a fight over the location of the territorial capital, which Tucson had lost to Prescott and wanted back. Locations would also be assigned for the territorial prison and the insane asylum. The capital location was a matter of civic pride; the asylum would offer the largest building and furnishing contracts.

J. S. Mansfeld of Tucson, a "leading citizen and active Republican," had proposed that Tucson seek to have a university established here ". . . and give up, once and for all, the fight over the capital and the territorial prison."[2] (The earlier Methodist proposal for a university is described in chapter 3.) However, as Franklin stated in his address, in a territory with a non-Indian population of forty thousand, not one high school, and a woefully inadequate grammar school system, the idea of a university ". . . did not impress the average citizen as a matter to be considered at all."[3]

From January through March of 1885, the Thirteenth Legislature brawled, bribed, and vote-swapped its way through one public issue after another. Had modern campaign and governmental laws been on the books and enforced, the practices Franklin described[4] would have caused virtually the entire body to be driven out of office, many to prison.

On the whole, things went badly for Tucson. It was decided that Prescott would remain the capital, Yuma would keep the prison, and Phoenix would get the asylum. Finally all that was left to decide on was a university for which few saw the need, and for which the Pima County delegation was in no position to bargain.

Franklin admitted that his actions had been part of the problem: "I had made many a fight against bills other members had introduced . . . leaving my pathway strewn with as many enemies as friends . . . . And [only] when it was too late did I appreciate how grievously could others retaliate upon me."[5]

In the vote-swapping frenzy of earlier days, a majority of the members of the upper house had committed themselves to the university bill. They passed it without enthusiasm in early March. It then became Franklin's responsibility to guide the bill through "an indifferent and to some extent hostile house." He was to address that house on behalf of the bill. Of this he said: "If the bill was to be passed at all, it was by votes . . . given without expectation of any return. It had to be passed by the force of argument or persuasion . . . by the power of speech alone."[6]

What Franklin remembers of that address is sketchy:

> Exactly what I said in that speech, other than to state the salient provisions of the bill, I do not recall except this:
>
> I told my associates that it was conceded that the 13th Legislature was the most energetic, the most contentious, and the most corrupt legislature that Arizona had had. We were called the fighting 13th, the bloody 13th, the thieving 13th, and we deserved these names, and we all knew it.
>
> We had employed so many clerks . . . that each member had one and a half clerks. We had subsidized the local press with extravagant appropriations so that our short comings should not be published . . . we had voted ourselves additional pay in violation of the Act of Congress.

> "But gentlemen," I said, "here is an opportunity to wash away our sins. Let us establish an institution of learning; let us pass this bill creating opportunities of education where they may learn to be better citizens than we are; and all our short comings will be forgotten in a misty past, and we will be remembered only for this one great achievement."[7]

Franklin recalled his own commencement at the University of California at Berkeley in 1882:

> I pictured to my associates the commencement days of our future University of Arizona, where the graceful maidens in white gowns and the stalwart youth, seated amidst bowers of flowers facing great stretches of green lawns on which the people had assembled, would raise their voices in praise of the glorious Thirteenth Legislature, which gave them the great opportunity of their lives . . . . "For your own salvation, gentlemen, you must vote for this bill."
>
> Then there arose applause, such as we had not heard in the house before. The lobbies cheered and stamped and clapped their hands . . . . [8]

The bill passed with one dissenting vote. The governor signed it into law on March 12, 1885. On the thirty-seventh anniversary of that event, Franklin told the story in the addressed I have just quoted.

This story illustrates the principles of identificational repentance and representative reconciliation (discussed in chapter 2) in action. Let's look at the pattern:

- An honest statement of indisputable facts.
- The identification of self with the problem. Again and again, "we" and not "you" is the pronoun used. There is an avoidance of self-righteous accusations.
- The statement of a need for restitution.
- An offer of hope for the future.
- Presentation of a feasible plan of action.

John Dawson, who has written and talked extensively about identificational repentance and representative reconciliation, has said, "The greatest authority will be gained by him who offers the greatest hope."[9] That proved true for Franklin. Revered as "the father of the University of Arizona," he remained a leading figure in Tucson until his death in 1926.

But are we dealing with Biblical principles here? Offering hope is certainly such a principle. The keynote of Biblical prophecy in both the Old and New Testaments is hope for the future under God's leadership.

The principles of identificational repentance and representative reconciliation can be found in several passages of the Bible—in the book of Judges, in Ezra 9 and 10, and in Nehemiah 1:6-7 and 9:1-38. These passages contain some or all of the elements described earlier. Old issues are dealt with, unity is achieved, and action is taken.

QUESTIONS FOR DISCUSSION

1. Is there a modern example, in either the religious community or the secular, of an attempt to put these principles into practice? Did the attempt succeed or fail?

2. The charm of Franklin's account contrasts with the dullness of most public discourse. Its candor contrasts with the self-righteousness of much of this discourse. What lessons could modern public figures draw from that? What lessons can you yourself draw from it?
3. On what issues do the American people most need offers of hope today? Who might offer that hope? How?
4. If the modern evangelical community took an "identification" approach more often, how might that affect outsiders' perception of the evangelical community?

NOTES TO CHAPTER 4

1 Selim M. Franklin, "Early History of the University of Arizona," March 12, 1922. The nine-page typescript is in Special Collections at the University of Arizona Library.
Of the written accounts of the early history of the University of Arizona, none is more complete or readable than Douglas Martin's Lamp in the Desert: The Story of the University of Arizona (Tucson: University of Arizona Press, 1960). Available in UA Special Collections.

2 Franklin, "Early History," _.

3 Ibid., 2.

4 Ibid., 2-6.

5 Ibid., 5.

6 Ibid., _.

7 Ibid., _.

8 Ibid., 5-6.

9 John Dawson, conference sponsored by Abundant Life Christian Center and Casas Adobes Baptist Church, Tucson, May 1993. See also Dawson's book Taking Our Cities for God: How to Break Spiritual Strongholds (Lake Mary, Fla.: Creation House, 1989).

chapter 6

DWIGHT L. MOODY'S CAMPAIGN IN TUCSON

We were in the midst of iniquity such as I never read of in a civilized land. I was real surprised that Mr. Moody at his advanced age should think of working there with as little prospect as there was.

Daniel B. Towner,

Moody campaign song leader, writing about Arizona

At the mining town of Tucson . . . Moody and Towner had to distribute the tickets themselves.

John C. Pollock

It is missionary ground and we will do the best we can.

Dwight L. Moody, 1899

In 1898-99, Dwight L. Moody, who for about twenty-five years had been the world's foremost Christian evangelist, went on a tour of the Western United States. It was an arduous task for the aging and ailing Moody. During the first few months of the tour, he was accompanied by wife Emma, son William, and song leader Daniel B. Towner.

In Arizona, Moody was scheduled to preach in Phoenix in mid-January for about two weeks, and one day at the territorial prison in Yuma (a state's largest correctional institution was usually part of Moody's itinerary.) Tucson was not scheduled on his tour.

It is doubtful that the Tucson evangelical community, as a whole, would have had the self-confidence to approach Moody about a Tucson campaign. As was discussed in chapter 3, it was a small community. Even estimating its size is difficult. It cannot be assumed that every Protestant church member was an evangelical. Nor can it be assumed that all evangelicals were communicant members of the Tucson churches. Serious evangelicals probably made up less than 10 percent of the population.

Some Tucsonans, though, had a bolder vision. Among them were the husband-and-wife editorial team of the Arizona Daily Star, Louis C. and Josephine Hughes. On January 8, 1899, the Star was so bold as to proclaim: "The coming of Evangelist Moody to Tucson suggests the importance of securing his services for a few days in Tucson. We cannot afford to have the opportunity pass . . ." (p. 2).

Moody began his Phoenix meetings on January 15. The public confirmation that he would be in Tucson appeared on page 1 of the Star on January 22, one week to the day before his scheduled arrival on Sunday, January 29. Song leader Daniel B. Towner would arrive in advance, on Friday, to begin rehearsing the choir. An editorial on page 2 of the same issue promoted the meetings, appealing to civic pride and the Tucson rivalry with Phoenix: "Phoenix has honored itself and the territory by the intense interest her people have taken . . . in [Moody's] good work in their midst. Tucson can do no less. We ought to do more."

The site of the meetings was the Tucson Opera House, located at 51 East Congress Street. Built by A. V. Grossetta and opened in 1897, it had the largest auditorium in Southern Arizona. "Then it was the most renowned and luxurious theater in the Southwest." Sarah Bernhardt and other major stars performed there in its heyday. According to the Phoenix Daily Herald, it could "seat 850 at ease or 1,000 crowded."[1]

On January 24, the Star reported that the choir was rehearsing each evening at the Methodist church. It exhorted its readers, "Let everyone who can sing join the choiristers, whether they belong to any church or not."

The rest of the Moody party actually arrived in Tucson by train from Colorado on Saturday, January 28. On that day Moody wrote the first of four letters to William Norton, head of the Bible Institute Colportage Association in Chicago.[2] Moody had founded this literature arm of his Bible Institute in 1894. This was done partly to provide tuition money for needy Bible Institute students (who did most of the sales work) and partly to distribute Moody's sermons and other Christian literature. Moody had been a salesman before going into religious work full-time. He seems to have relished the opportunity to again be involved in the direct sale of a product; he personally did the work at every opportunity.[3]

On Sunday, January 29, a Star editorial said of Moody, "He comes to do us good, he comes without price to give us his best thought, his highest and purest aspirations . . ." (p. 2). The Star's rival newspaper, the Tucson Daily Citizen, virtually ignored Moody's presence. Only one paragraph, containing notably faint praise for the evangelist, appeared while he was in town (on February 1).

The January 31 Star covered the first two days of the campaign. It reported that the Sunday afternoon sermon was entitled "Rest," the evening sermon "Sowing and Reaping." There was a lengthy synopsis of the latter message: "The deliverance of the evangelist was well suited to the present conditions of Tucson. [Moody] spoke fearlessly of the evils in our midst . . . violation of the sabbath, the saloon traffic, the gambling trade . . . . How could Tucson sow these crops and expect other than vice, crime, and destruction? . . . [H]e spoke in kindness of those who were doing the sowing. He pled for them to seek and go into a better business."

An editorial on page 2 of the same issue described crowds at the evening meetings as "the largest evening audiences ever seated in the house." Page 4 had a brief account of Monday's sermons, "The Filling of the Spirit" and "The New Birth."

An editorial entitled "Think on This" appeared on page 2 of the February 1 issue of the Star. It described the meetings as "the most sought after of any public gatherings in Tucson." Moody's work was compared to that of the early Southwestern Catholic padres, which had had an impact on the life and culture of Arizona. The comparison of Moody to the Catholic missionaries was a natural one for Hughes. Both of Tucson's papers often reported Catholic Church news. In 1903, the illness and death of Pope Leo XIII and the accession of Pius X would be front-page news for many days.

Nor was Moody likely to have been offended. His attitude toward Catholicism differed from the intolerance of many evangelicals of his time.[4] The Phoenix-based Arizona Republican (now the Arizona Republic) had noted this on January 16 and had quoted an anecdote in a Ladies' Home Journal article: "When asked officiously when he was going to preach against the

Catholics, he answered, 'Just as soon as all the Protestants are converted.'"[5] James F. Findlay, Jr., reports that when the Catholic parish in Moody's home town and headquarters, Northfield, Massachusetts, built a new building, he made a financial contribution to the project. This infuriated some of his friends and colleagues.[6]

The February 1 issue of the Star devoted a full column on page 2 to a virtually complete synopsis of the Tuesday evening sermon, "Excuses." The text for that sermon was Luke 14:18-20. The Wednesday evening sermon, "Christ Seeking Sinners," was reported on page 1 of the February 2 issue. The text that evening was Luke 19:10.

From the Star's glowing reports, one would never have guessed that difficulties were mounting day by day. Although the populace was willing enough to attend the meetings, they were evidently not willing to do the chores and legwork required to make such meetings really successful. Moody and Towner had to distribute the tickets to the meetings. Also, Moody's books did not sell in Tucson.

Moody's frustration can be seen in comments he made in letter to Norton back home. In an undated letter he wrote: "This is a hard old town one of the worst we have . . . any where and they do not read so I do not know how I am to get on . . . but it is missionary ground and we will do the best we can." In a letter dated February 2 he stated: I am leaving 300 col [portage] books with Rochester Ford. He is a lawyer but he is going to try to get someone to sell them."

Ford and Moody had apparently become fast friends. They were in close proximity during Moody's stay in Tucson. Since Moody wrote his letters to Norton on Hotel San Augustine stationery, it might be inferred that he stayed there. The hotel building had been Tucson's Roman Catholic cathedral until the new (and present) Saint Augustine Cathedral was consecrated in 1897. It was located at 43 South Stone. Ford's **[home? office?]** was located at 36 South Stone.[7]

Ford was the only Tucsonan mentioned by name in Moody's letters. His offer of help was a bright spot in what was rapidly becoming a fiasco. The cruelest blow came when the week of meetings had to be cut short. About the time Moody arrived in town, it was learned that the Opera House was engaged for the following Saturday and Sunday. It was then planned to hold the last meeting Friday afternoon. But late Thursday word came that the group engaging the Opera House needed it Friday afternoon as well. So the Thursday evening meeting would be the last.[8]

On top of every other difficulty, it rained Thursday evening. This affected attendance, but the Star gallantly reported that the crowd was "very much larger than could have been expected in Tucson." The sermon that night was entitled "Thou Art Not Far from the Kingdom of God." Afterward came an extended time of counseling inquirers. The meeting concluded with the singing of "God Be with You till We Meet Again." The Star stated that the Moody party was to leave by train for Yuma on Friday morning. There they would conduct a service at the territorial prison, then leave Arizona for Colton, California.[9]

Why did Moody encounter so many difficulties in Tucson? One of the obvious factors was the haste with which the Tucson arrangements had been made. Everything had been done over a period of a few days, or at most a few weeks. The Opera House debacle suggests that local efforts combined haste with carelessness.

The chief promoter of the Moody effort, L. C. Hughes, had publicly expressed religious views so at variance with what conservative evangelicals believe (see chapter 6) that one wonders whether they fully trusted him, much less considered them one of their own. Whatever their confidence in Moody, their view of Moody's chief promoter in Tucson may have influenced their view of the campaign itself.

Dwight L. Moody died on December 22, 1899, six weeks after being stricken while preaching in Kansas City, Kansas. The lead editorial of the December 24 Star was a lengthy tribute to him. Near the end of that editorial, a startling claim is made: "[Moody's] visit to Arizona and his work, especially in Tucson, determined him to return here this winter . . . he wanted to save Arizona. His big heart was set on Tucson. It was his intention to pitch a large Gospel tent on the plaza and make a winter's campaign here . . . ." That seems to reflect a change of heart from the sentiments Moody had expressed about Tucson in his letter to Norton. The Moody Bible Institute has no information to corroborate the report that he planned a return visit to Tucson.

There are four possible solutions to this mystery:

1. Moody communicated his desire to return to someone in Tucson, but not to his own associates. The "someone" would almost certainly have been the Hugheses or Ford. However, virtually no personal correspondence of either is extant in Tucson. Therefore, this theory is untestable.
2. Moody informed his associates of his desire to return to Tucson but did not publicize it, and they dropped the matter after his death. Daniel Towner's opinion of Arizona was, if anything, lower than Moody's.

3. The Hugheses misunderstood Moody's intention. This theory is also untestable, also because of a lack of documentary evidence.
4. The Hugheses fabricated the entire story. This is another untestable theory. But it should be noted that the sizable body of literature on this couple contains no evidence that they were in the habit of lying in print.

The reader is free to make his or her own judgment as to the validity of these options or to propose another. The author would like to know the truth of the matter.

Despite the difficulties the Moody party encountered in Tucson and the negative opinions about the city and the state that they expressed privately, it says a great deal about them that they were willing to work in a place where no financial support appeared to be forthcoming and prospects of tangible results were bleak. In addition, the Moodys were working in the midst of crushing personal tragedy. They had been presented with four grandchildren by their son William and his wife. A son, D. L.'s namesake, had died on November 30, 1898, at the age of one year. Little D. L.'s sister Irene was ill, first with pneumonia and then with tuberculosis. Irene and her mother joined the Moody party some weeks after the Arizona meetings. It was hoped that the warmer climate of the West would improve Irene's condition. Instead, though, she died on August 22, 1899, at the age of four.

William Moody later wrote: "Mr. Moody's own deep affliction in the bereavement was hidden from the parents in his unselfish efforts to cheer them."[10] Many observers believed that this grief, combined with Moody's own physical problems, mentioned earlier, led to the evangelist's physical collapse and subsequent death less than a year after his Tucson visit.

Only eternity will reveal what good ultimately came of the unselfish efforts of the Moody party. In the words of Jesus, "Here the saying holds true, 'One sows and another reaps . . . .' Others have labored and you have entered into their labor" (John 4:37-38).

Copies of Moody's letters from Tucson (or from any other city in which he preached on his final tour, including Phoenix) can be obtained from the library of the Moody Bible Institute, 820 North La Salle Drive, Chicago, Illinois 60610. The only charge will be for copying and postage.

QUESTIONS FOR DISCUSSION

1. Would you call Moody's Tucson campaign a success or a failure? Why?
2. Do you think Moody really intended to return to Tucson? If not, why did the Star editors believe he did?
3. Compare the significance of outstanding individuals in American church history with the significance of "ordinary" active Christians, both clergy and lay.
4. From what you have read here, would you say that the Hugheses and others were relying on God to do great things through Moody and his hearers, or relying on Moody himself to do great things? How might their expectations have influenced the course and the outcome of the meetings?
5. Conflicting agendas.

NOTES TO CHAPTER 6

1 In 1918, the Tucson Opera House became a movie theater. It was torn down in 1986 and replaced by a parking garage that has approximately the same dimensions.

2 James F. Findlay, Jr., Dwight L. Moody: American Evangelist, 1837-1899 (Chicago: University of Chicago Press, 1969), 398-99.

3 Ibid., 418.

4 He once said, "I hope . . . to see the day when all bickering, division, and party spirit will cease, and Roman Catholics will see eye to eye with Protestants in this work. Let us advance . . . Roman Catholics, Protestant . . . against the rants of Satan's emissaries." Findlay, Moody, 248.

5 The exact issue of the Ladies' Home Journal in which this appeared could not be determined. The magazine itself does not have issues dated prior to 1900 in its archives.

6 Findlay, Moody, 371-72.

7 Addresses from the Tucson City Directory, 1901, p. _.

8 Arizona Daily Star, February 2, 1899.

9 Arizona Daily Star, February 3, 1899, p. 1.

10 William Moody, The Life of Dwight L. Moody (New York: Fleming H. Revell, 1900), 537-41.

chapter 7

TOUCHING THE "UNTOUCHABLES"

O. E. Comstock in Tentville

> You are the salt of the earth . . . . You are the light of the world . . . . Let your light shine before men, that they may see your good deeds and praise your Father in heaven.
>
> —Matthew 5:13-16

> When the darkness is the worst, the light can shine the best.

In the early part of the last century, a great darkness surrounded the disease tuberculosis (TB), as well as those with the disease and their families. TB was incurable and hard to treat. An early death awaited most who contracted it. The best one could hope for was that the disease would be arrested so that he or she might live a normal life span.

Public attitudes added to the suffering of victims and families. TB inspired much the same kind of fear that AIDS does today. It was thought to be even more highly contagious than it was. Those with the disease—and often their families—were feared and shunned as if they were lepers or India's "untouchables."

People with TB had to live in isolated areas, such as Tucson's Tentville. Tentville—so named for the modified tent-framed dwellings of which it was comprised—was located outside the city limits, north of Speedway. It extended from North First Avenue to Campbell. Hundreds of people at a time lived in these dwellings. Life in Tentville is poignantly described by Dick Hall, who grew up there, in an article in Journal of Arizona History.1

There were treatment facilities in the Tentville area for those who had the money for treatment. Most didn't. The effect on family life of sickness, poverty, and frequently the permanent separation of spouses was devastating. Most outsiders—including most church members—shunned this community. Small wonder that the suicide rate among victims was astronomical.

Some of those with TB must have wondered if even God had forgotten them. He hadn't. In 1907, Oliver E. Comstock came to Tucson from Alabama with his wife, Jennie, and their children.[2] The Comstocks were TB refugees; one of their children had the disease. Comstock had for many years been a bivocational Baptist preacher and printer. He had also held public office and edited a newspaper. Now, at age 53, he had to start over.

Comstock did well in Tucson. With a partner he built a successful printing business. He served two terms as a justice of the peace and on the Tucson City Council, and he was a member of the First Baptist Church.

God soon gave Comstock a burden for the TB community. In 1909, he started a Sunday School for patients and their families. In 1910, he bought a house in the 1000 block of East Adams Street, in the heart of Tentville, and moved the Sunday School there. The Adams Street Mission served the Tentville community as long as that community existed.

A few years later, the suicide of an impoverished person with TB moved Comstock to start a free hospital for people with TB. It opened in 1915 on the Adams Street property. First called Mercy Emergency Hospital, its name was soon changed to Comstock Hospital. It was the only free hospital in town. There the Comstocks and volunteer medical personnel cared for as many as sixty patients at a time. It was several years before they could afford a full-time nurse, much less a doctor, on staff.

The people of Tucson rallied behind the hospital. In 1919, the first permanent building was erected with private donations, the largest $100, and with volunteer labor. Two years later, another wing was built. The hospital began to care for impoverished war veterans and transients in addition to patients with TB.[3] Eventually control passed out of Comstock's hands, but he continued to be associated with the hospital until his death in 1937.

Other Christian groups brought the same spirit. In 1917, the Episcopal Church opened Saint Luke's Hospital, also on Adams Street, for indigent men. It is still in operation, now as a retirement home for women.

Life and treatment facilities for TB patients improved. In the 1920s, to no one's regret, Tentville disappeared. The Veterans Administration and Country Hospitals were founded. That left only needy children for Comstock Hospital to care for. In 1966, Comstock Children's Hospital was closed. The building now houses the University of Arizona School of Health-

Related Professions. The Comstock Foundation continues as a secular charity that provides financial and advocacy services to needy families with sick children.

QUESTIONS FOR DISCUSSION

1. Who are some modern "untouchables"? Is the evangelical community following Comstock's example in reaching out to them? Or does it tend to shun them and add to their isolation?
2. Was the evolution of the Comstock organization from Christian ministry to secular charity a sign of failure on the part of the evangelical community? Or was God merely calling that community to move on to something else?

SUGGESTIONS FOR FURTHER RESEARCH

The number of children who grew up in Tentville is rapidly decreasing as these people age and die. This suggests the urgency of locating and interviewing them. Might their stories, along with further historical research on the situation in which they grew up, be the makings of a book-length manuscript?

chapter 8

ETHNIC EVANGELICALS

AFRICAN AMERICANS, PART I

How local African-Americans gathered for worship prior to 1900 has not been satisfactorily documented. Did they gather in homes? Were they ever allowed to worship with the predominantly white congregations?

Once a substantial community of African-American Protestant women existed, African-American churches began to be formed. By 1905, a community that numbered, at most, 150 persosn was supporting three churches!

The first was organized in 1900, by 10 persons. It was originally called Baptist Mission. The first pastor was a denominational missionary, Rev. Bell (first name unknown.) He was succeeded in 1901 by Rev. Vance M. Cole. The congregation was renamed Second Baptist Church. In 1910, the present name, Mount Calvary Missionary Baptist Church, was adopted.

In 1903, Rev. Cole and his wife and children were received as full members by First Methodist. It was then very unusual for an African-American family to be so received by a white congregation. (First Methodist also had some Hispanic and Asian members.)

Shortly afterward, there appeared in the1903-04 Pima County, A.T. Directory a congregation listed as the "African Methodist" Church, V.M. Cole, Pastor. No African-American history source I have consulted mentions this congregation.

Cole was a businessman through whom the white establishment worked when dealing with African-Americans. Rightly or wrongly, he was, and still is regarded by some, as an "Uncle Tom." Some other early African-American ministers were also distrusted for a variety of reasons.

The "African Methodist" Church appears through the 1916 City Directory. That is also the last year that V. M. Cole appears. His 13-year pastorate was the second longest in the frontier period. But it did not produce a lasting congregation. That may illustrate the often-made point that too close and long-lasting a relationship between "mother church" and "daughter church" is not a good thing. Perhaps it also indicates that the rapid turnover of pastors in the other churches was a "blessing in disguise:" It forced the members to rely on themselves, not on the "man up front."

In 1905, Prince Chapel African Methodist Episcopal Church was organized in the kitchen of Rev. Ratcliff Hughes, the first pastor.

The work of Dr. Harry Lawson, and of his associates and successors in the African American History Project of Pima Community College, is of inestimable improtance to the study of Tucson church history. The 1990 volume on African-American churches, listed below, is one of the few interdenominational studies of Tucson church history.

THE APACHES

Given the prevailing attitude toward the Apaches, the wonder is that anyone had the courage to undertake missionary work among them.

Tucson was founded as a refuge from Apache raids, and as a staging area for attacks upon them. For two centuries, life in the Old Pueblo centered on the struggle with the Apache. They were feared and hated by Anglos, Hispanics, and most other Native Americans.

The tribe had six major divisions, each with its own leaders. Not to mention the occasional band of renegades, who raided without anyone's authorization. This made it impossible for anyone to speak for the whole tribe, or to exercise restraint on the whole.

These complexities were lost on most outsiders. To them, all Apaches were responsible for the actions of any. Almost everyone knew someone who had been killed by some group of Apaches. And most wanted all Apaches to pay for it.

Jo Conners, in Who's Who in Arizoan (1913,) describes the prevailing attitude on p. 13-14. He gives, without censure, an anonymous quote from a "prominent person forty years ago." From the style, it was probably John Wasson, Editor of the Citizen:

"The Apaches can neither be Christianized nor civilized. They are the one tribe which refused the cross from good old Father Kino in 1670* nor have they accepted it since that time."

There followed a verbose assertion that settlement and industry could not develop in Arizona until they were completely exterminated. This was the view of most Anglos, an even larger majority of Mexican-Americans, and of many rival Native Americans. The removal of some Apachesin the 1880s first to Florida, then to Oklahoma, is deplored by many today. But by the standard of the times, it was a "moderate" solution to the Apache problem.

*Kino did not arrive in the region until the 1680s.

The further from O'odham country one went, the more the terms "Apache" and "Indian" became synonymous in the public mind. While the French were naming gangsters and dances after the Apache, an Austrian boy named Adolf Hitler was reading trashy "Western" novels, in which the Apaches were depicted as subhumans, fit only for extermination. How might this reading have influenced his later thinking?

In this context, the infamous Camp Grant Massacre is not surprising. Here, in brief, are the facts:

In April, 1871, there were some Apache raids in the east central part of Arizoan. Rumor had it that the Arivaipa Apaches, under Chief Eskiminzen, were responsible. This band had earlier been on the warpath, but had abandoned fighting and settled peacefully on their land in the White Mountains, under the protection of the U. S. Army, engaging in agriculture and receiving instruction in Christianity from a Presbyterian missionary.

The rumor reached Tucson. John Wasson used the Citizen to whip up a frenzy for revenge. At the end of April, a revenge raid was secretly planned by prominent Tucsonans. The raiding party consisted of six Anglos, 42 Mexican-Americans, and 92 Tohono O'odham. They slipped out of town, travelling by night to avoid detection by the Army.

They arrived at the Apache camp at dawn. Most of the men of the village were out hunting and gathering agave leaves. This made the raiders' task easier. The O'odham attacked the camp, and the Anglos and Mexicans formed a circle around it, and shot any who tried to escape. Of the more than 100 Apaches killed, only eight were adult males. The O'odham carried off 27 children as captives.

The Citizen and other Western newspapers praised the raid. Eastern newspapers and periodicals denounced it as a "massacre."

THE TOHONO O'ODHAM

This tribe maintained a peaceful and cooperative relationship with the whites. They even grew wheat for the Army during and after the Civil War period. Therefore, they had no treaty to protect their rights, and no reservation. As time wore on, they were robbed blind by the mining and cattle interests. They were reduced to destitution. Few Anglos had the courage to fight these interests.

Among the few were the Presbyterian missionaries who ran the Tucson Indian School, and who founded a church which would eventually become Southside Presbyterian Church. In cooperation with the Indian agent, Cato Sells, (for whom the town of Sells, Ariz. is named,) they foughtvaliantly for their rights. Largely through their efforts, a tribal government was formed, and in 1916, a reservation finally obtained. Extensive first-hand accounts of these events are housed in the Arizona Historical Society Library.

THE MEXICAN-AMERICANS

Work among them began early. In the 1880s, the Episcopalians had some Mexican-American members. In 1888, a Spanish Methodist congregation was established. By 1912, there was a Spanish language Baptist church.

THE CHINESE

Again, the Episcopalians took the lead, receiving some Chinese members in the 1880s. By 1912, the Chinese Evangelical Church had been organized, under Baptist auspices.

THE JEWS

Tucson's Jewish community was prosperous and highly respected. In 1883, both the mayor and the chief of police were Jewish. As were several of the prime movers behind the location of the University of Arizona in Tucson. A number of the Jewish men married into prominent non-Jewish families. Grace Episcopal Church, in particular, had a large number of families headed by Jewish men. Some eventually embraced Christianity, but most never did. Abe Chanin and his associates have written extensively about this community.

I know of no formal mission effort directed toward this community. In fact, I would be surprised to learn of any. These people were of great importance economically and politically, and had great respect as public benefactors. Such an outreach would have seemed very intimidating.

chapter 9

BRING IT HOME, CARRY IT FORWARD!

A POSSIBLE EVANGELICAL HISTORY SOCIETY

Those whom God calls to work in the area of Tucson evangelical history need a rallying point and a gathering place—an evangelical history society.

Such an organization would, of necessity, start small. It would have a small (five- to seven-member) board, with a chairperson. At first, most work and contact would be informal. The constitution might require as little as one meeting per year. Holding meetings infrequently might prevent the burnout that is so common in small, struggling organizations.

As more people were added to the society, it could meet more often and do more formal work. It could make contacts with churches and ministries and with the secular historical community. It might eventually become a certified historical society under ARS-41-821-h and become affiliated with the Arizona Historical Society. This would be mutually beneficial.

MINDSETS OF THE PAST, PRESENT, AND FUTURE

Frontier society demonstrated a mindset that differed from the mindset of today and will certainly differ as well from that of the future. The mindset of frontier society, perpetuated in elite circles until the 1960s or even later, misunderstood the past, deprecated the present, and lived for the future. The mindset of our society, on the other hand, deprecates the past, lives for the present, and distrusts the future.

Playing past, present, and future against each other, as our society does today, has resulted in discontinuity. If we want to promote continuity in the future, we must develop a mindset that harmonizes past, present, and future. We must understand and respect the past; live in, act in, and value the present; and look toward and plan for the future.

Residents of Tucson have long wanted our community to "be like" communities of the East Coast or the West Coast. Therefore, we have tried to emulate models we didn't really understand and weren't equipped to duplicate, models that weren't really appropriate for us to begin with. We have simultaneously prided ourselves on our supposed distinctiveness and sought to obliterate distinctions.

It is now clear that we must understand the sacredness of the present day and preserve the sacred things that happen today for the people who will come after us.

The struggles, successes, and failures of our forebears can be a great source of hope and encouragement for us. Those who went before us faced hardships and difficulties. They experienced disappointments and frustrations. They suffered losses. But they stuck with it. They endured, survived, and left a heritage for their children and their children's children. If they did that, why can't we?

The God who guided them also guides us. Unless we treasure God's gifts of the past and understand and utilize His gifts of the present, we will miss out on the future He longs to give us.

There was an outward display of unity and harmony among the various evangelical communities in early Tucson. But it was always displayed in the face of some real or imagined enemy. At first the enemy was the Apache. Then the three peoples turned on each other. Then the enemy became either those who stood in the way of "progress" or those whose idea of progress threatened entrenched groups. More and more, the unity became that of factions uniting against each other to fight wars among them.

What if a new unity could be forged—a unity built around the premise that, though diverse, we are one people?

Secularists—and religious liberals, for that matter—decry the Biblical teachings on Satan and demons. But those teachings have some advantages.

THE LEGACY OF THE EARLY PERIOD

It was not for the impatient, the timid, the pessimistic, or the easily distracted. Tangible results were meager and slow in coming. But over time, the work paid off.

One of the things the study of history points to is the sacredness of the present moment. To see how people lived their "present moments," and to trace the long-term consequences, good and bad, of how they used those moments, tell us a lot about them. But they also speak to us about our use of our present moments. If we are tempted to disregard the here and now, to disdain what we have or what we are, we can see what doing so cost our forebears—and us—and perhaps behave differently ourselves.

Suppose that, instead of building walls to "protect" some of us from the rest of us, we built them to protect all of us.

Suppose that the "enemy" we resisted was not a group of people, but the spiritual and intellectual forces of evil and disruption.

Suppose we understood that we are "all in the same boat" in many ways, that we have been placed together here, in this city, for our mutual benefit and that of the city.

We lost our past, and with it we lost each other. Or, perhaps more accurately, we lost our past without ever having found each other. If we can find our past together, perhaps we can find each other again, together.

We stand to gain far more than we ever lost. If all the theological, denominational, economic, and ethnic groups could know each other's histories—what we all have in common, and what is unique about each—we could know each other in the present and could live and minister in fellowship with God and each other in the present and in the future.

Acts of mercy and social action are not evangelism. They can never substitute for evangelism. But they can greatly aid evangelism. They build credibility for both the Good News and its messengers. The folly of separating one from the other is evident from how they were combined in this period of Tucson church history.

But afterward they became separated in the minds of too many Christians and churches. Some ran with evangelism, with only a little charitable work to draw in evangelistic prospects. Such churches often became suspicious of

Other churches ran with mercy and social action. Not only did they tend to deemphasize evangelism; they often refused to cooperate with, and even openly attacked, community-wide evangelistic efforts.

THE UNITY OF PERSONAL AND SOCIAL ETHICS

The evangelicals of this time and place understood that one must have both a personal and a social ethic, and that each should complement and reinforce the other.

READING LIST

TUCSON HISTORY

The Best:

C. L. Sonnichesen, *Tucson: The Life and Times of an American City* (______________: Universtiy of Oklahoma Press, 1982).

Also:

Howard W. Billman, *A Crown of Thorns: The Reward of a University of Arizona President* (Tucson: ______________).

Julie A. Campbell, Linda M. Gregonis, Robert F. Pamquist, and Charles W. Polzen, S.J.

O. E. Comstock, Clippings Files, Arizona Historical Society Library, Tucson.

Southwestern Mission Research Center, *Tucson: A Short History* (______________: Southwestern Mission Research Center, 1986).

Rochester Ford, Rochester Ford file, Special Collections, University of Arizona Main Library, Tucson.

Selim M. Franklin, the Selim Franklin Letters (82 boxes containing hundreds of letters and other materials), Special Collections, University of Arizona Main Library, Tucson.

Douglas D. Martin, *A Lamp in the Desert: The Story of the University of Arizona* (Tucson: University of Arizona Press, 1960). Available in UA Special Collections.

On the Tucson Hispanic Community:

Thomas E. Sheridan, *Los Tucsonenses: The Mexican-American Community in Tucson, 1854-1941* (Tucson: University of Arizona Press, 1986).

THE TUCSON NATIVE AMERICAN COMMUNITY

Don Schellie, *Vast Domain of Blood: The Story of the Camp Grant Massacre* (Los Angeles: Westernlore Press, 1968).

Edward Spicer, Cycles of Conquest.

THE TUCSON AFRICAN-AMERICAN COMMUNITY:

Harry H. Lawson

African-American History Project

THE ROMAN CATHOLIC CHURCH IN TUCSON

For a brief history of the Diocese of Tucson see also http://www.diocesetucson.org/welcome.html.

THE JEWISH COMMUNITY IN TUCSON

Abe Chanin,

chapter 10

ONE CHURCH'S STORY

First Baptist

USE OF THE WORD *HOPE* IN THE BIBLE

In *Strong's Concordance* to the King James Version of the Bible, the word *hope* appears 127 times, 69 in the Old Testament and 58 in the New Testament; *hoped* appears 11 times, 7 in the Old Testament and 4 in the New Testament. *Hope* appears 16 times in Job, 22 in Psalms, 7 in Proverbs, and 13 in Romans.

The word makes its first appearance in Ruth 1:12, in which the author expresses a hopelessness that God turned around. After that it appears as follows:

Ezra 10:2—". . . yet now there is hope in Israel [that God will rectify a bad mistake] . . . ."

Job 4:6—

Psalm 16:9—"rest secure."

22:9—"hope" (the New International Version [NIV] has "trust").

31:24—

33:18, 22—". . . hope in . . . his unfailing love" (the King James Version [KJV] has "mercy" [hesed?]).

38:15—"wait"

42:5, 11—". . . put your hope in God."

43:5—for the third time in two Psalms, "Why so downcast . . . ? Put your hope in God."

71:5, 14—". . . you have been my . . . I will always have hope."

78:7—"hope" (the NIV has "trust").

119:49, 81, 114, 116, 49—". . . you have given me hope"; "I put my hope in your word"; ". . . . do not let my hopes be dashed."

130:5, 7—". . . in his word I put my hope"; ". . . put your hope in the Lord."

131:3—". . . put your hope in the Lord."

146:5—". . . hope is in the Lord his God."

147:11—". . . put their hope in his unfailing love" (hesed).

Prov. 10:28—". . . hopes of the wicked come to nothing."

11:7—". . . wicked dies, hope perishes."

13:12—"Hope deferred makes the heart sick."

14:32—"hope" (the NIV has "refuge").

19:18—". . . discipline your son, for in that there is hope."

26:12—". . . wise in his own eyes? . . . more hope for a fool . . . ."

29:20—". . . speaks in haste? . . . . more hope for a fool."

Eccl. 9:4—"Anyone who is among the living has hope."

Isaiah 38:18—"The dead . . . cannot hope for your faithfulness."

Hezekiah—

Isaiah 57:10—"hopeless" (NIV)

Jer. 2:25—"It's no use!"

14:8—"O Hope of Israel . . ."

17.7—"confidence"

17:13—"O Lord, the hope of Israel"

17:17—"refuge"

18:12—"It's no use!"

31:17—"So there is hope for your future."

50:7—". . . the Lord, the hope of their fathers."

Lament. 3:18—". . . all that I had hoped from the Lord."

3:24—". . . wait for Him" (NIV)

3:26—"wait"

3:29—". . . there may yet be hope."

Ezek. 13:6—"expect" (NIV)

19:5—"expectation"

37:11—". . . our hope is gone . . ."

Hosea 2:15—". . . a door of hope."

Joel 3:16—"a refuge" (NIV)

Zech. 9:12—". . . prisoners of hope."

Luke 6:34—"expect" (NIV)

Acts 2:26—". . . my body also will live in hope."

16:19—". . . their hope of making money . . ."

23:6—". . . my hope in the resurrection . . ."

24:15—". . . the same hope in God . . . resurrection . . ."

26:6—". . . my hope in what God has promised . . ."

26:7—". . . hoping to see, fulfilled . . ."

27:20—". . . gave up all hope . . ."

28:20—". . . because of the hope of Israel . . ."

ελπιοι—elpioi—el-pe-e Character produces hope!

δοκιμισ—dokimi—character

Romans 4:18—"Against all hope, Abraham in hope believed . . ."

5:2—". . . we rejoice in hope . . ."

5:4—". . . and character, character produces hope . . ."

5:5—". . . and hope does not disappoint . . ."

8:20—". . . in hope that the creation itself will be liberated"

8:21—"four 'hopes'"

8:24—"For in this hope we were saved. But hope that is seen is no hope at all. Who hopes for what he already has?"

8:25—". . . if we hope for what we do not yet have . . ."

12:12—"Be joyful in hope . . ."

15:4—". . . through . . . the Scriptures, we might have hope."

15:13—"May the God of hope fill you . . . that you may overflow with hope."

1 Cor. 9:10—". . . in the hope of sharing in the harvest."

"plow in hope," "thresh in hope." (KJV)

13:13—". . . faith, hope, and love." (NIV)

15:19—". . . if only in this life we have hope in Christ . . ."

2 Cor. 1:7—". . . our hope for you is firm . . ."

3:12—". . . since we have such a hope."

10:15—"our hope is that . . . our ministry . . . will expand."

Gal. 5:5—"We wait . . . through the Spirit the righteousness for which we hope."

Eph. 1:18—". . . the hope to which he has called you."

2:12—". . . without hope and without God . . ."

4:4—". . . called to one hope . . ."

Philip. 1:20—"I . . . hope that I will in no way be ashamed . . ."

2:23—"I hope . . . to send him . . ."

Col. 1:5—". . . the faith and love that spring from the hope . . ."

1:23—". . . not removed from the hope . . . in the Gospel."

1:27—". . . Christ in you, the hope of glory."

1 Thes. 1:3—". . . endurance inspired by hope in our Lord Jesus Christ."

2:19—". . . our hope, our joy, our crown."

4:13—". . . like the rest of men, who have no hope."

5:8—". . . the hope of salvation as our helmet."

2 Thes. 2:16—". . . gave us eternal encouragement and good hope."

1 Tim. 1:1—". . . Christ Jesus our hope."

Titus 1:2—". . . the hope of eternal life . . ."

2:13—". . . the blessed hope . . . the . . . appearing of . . . Jesus Christ"

3:7—". . . heirs having . . . the hope of eternal life."

Heb. 3:6—". . . the hope of which we boast."

6:11—". . . in order to make your hope sure."

6:18—". . . to take hold of the hope . . ."

6:19—". . . this hope is an anchor . . ."

7:19—". . . and a better hope . . ."

1 Peter 1:3—". . . new birth into a living hope . . ."

1:13—". . . set your hope fully on the grace . . ."

1:21—". . . your faith and hope are in God."

3:15—". . . reason for the hope that you have . . ."

1 John 3:3—"Everyone who has this hope . . . purifies himself . . ."

JOY CAME IN THE MORNING: THE EARLY HISTORY OF FIRST BAPTIST CHURCH AND WHAT IT MEANS TODAY

Scriptures: Psalm 126, Hebrews 12:1-2

Principle: Just as every Christian should know his spiritual history and be prepared to testify to it, so should every congregation and ministry. That history—that testimony—gives us guidance as to what we should do now and in the future.

The first evangelical Christians arrived in Tucson soon after the Gadsden Purchase of 1854. But they were a small minority within an overwhelmingly Catholic town and region. And so they remained throughout the frontier period.

It took years for Protestant churches to be formed. Protestants were not only few in number, but divided into many denominational backgrounds. Also, the Indian and Civil Wars disrupted everyone's religious life. In 1865 there was not one full-time Christian worker, Catholic or Protestant, ministering in Arizona. The remoteness of the area and a shortage of funds also hampered efforts.

But slowly things came together. From about 1870, Protestant services were occasionally held in Tucson. In 1878 the first Protestant congregation was formed. Meanwhile, Baptist life was getting organized in Prescott to the north; in January 1880 Arizona's first Baptist congregation, Lone Star Baptist (now First Baptist Church of Prescott) was organized.

Tucson was not far behind. In March 1881 the American Baptist Home Mission Society sent the Reverend Uriah Gregory and his wife, Alice, to town to start a church. Within a month a church had been organized and property purchased at the corner of Stone and Council. For many years First Baptist Church was a mission congregation. Later things came full circle; it would in turn organize and sponsor mission congregations.

On May 15, 1881, the inaugural service of First Baptist Church was held in the Presbyterian church building. The *Arizona Weekly* (soon to become the *Arizona Daily Star*) reported: "The services were very impressive and mark an era of Christian civilization in our ancient and honorable pueblo, from which we shall look forward hopefully to progress under the banner of the cross . . . ." That is what you could read in our morning paper in those days!

For the next year, while their building was under construction, the congregation met at various locations. In the summer, during the frontier period, the Protestant churches would hold a united service on Sunday nights, usually on someone's lawn. I am amazed at the unity displayed by the churches in those days.

The building went slowly. Money was scarce. The Gregorys mortgaged their house, and an Episcopalian woman from the East donated $500. Finally, it was completed.

That first year also witnessed the death of the Gregorys' four-year-old daughter and that of the president of the church's trustees. Those were the first of many tragedies the people of First Baptist Church would endure in the early years.

Otherwise, things went well for a while. The railroad's coming in 1880 brought unprecedented prosperity. And Tucson had long been a trade and mining center. The Gregorys gathered what seemed like a thriving congregation.

But then a crisis hit. And it went on year after year. We don't know all of the causes. But we do know that the railroad boom went bust in the late 1880s. Tucson's population dropped from 7,000 in 1880 to 5,000 in 1890. Add to that a terrible drought in Arizona and a nationwide depression, and it painted a bleak picture externally.

But what about internally? From 1890 to 1895, First Baptist Church had no pastor. After that, there were ten pastors in twenty-three years. Many came for their health, and two died while serving. There are hints in the scarce records of friction between Baptists of Northern and Southern backgrounds. Of course that wound is still festering within the memories of some who are still alive.

The worst year was 1890. First Baptist Church had only twenty members left. No services were being held regularly. The adobe building was not being maintained. All over Arizona, churches were closing their doors. Satan was obviously working to add First Baptist to the list.

But God had other ideas. In that awful year of 1890, a young attorney from Saint Louis came to Tucson for his health. His name was Rochester Ford. His parents were both nationally known Baptist leaders. He quickly became one of the most popular and influential citizens of Tucson (see chapter 4 for more on Ford).

Ford soon felt led to gather the few remaining members of First Baptist and resume regular services. Often he would preach himself. Another man who frequently served as preacher was the superintendent of the Tucson Indian School, a Presbyterian minister. As I said earlier, the churches were more united then than they are today.

Rochester Ford was named deacon and Sunday School superintendent of First Baptist. He paid to have the building repaired and the interior renovated. He was clearly the man God used to keep the doors open. And in the late 1890s a young people's group and a women's missionary group were formed.

Ford helped other ministries as well. Dwight L. Moody preached in Tucson for five days in 1899. In Moody's letters from Tucson, Ford is the only Tucsonan mentioned by name.

In 1903, Rochester Ford died. His parents, both of whom survived him, continued to send advice and financial help to First Baptist.

The congregation struggled on. Progress was slow and unsteady. During the 1903-04 church year, membership dropped from sixty-three to fifty-seven. There were two baptisms that year—the same number as in 1998, by the way.

On top of everything, in 1905 the city condemned the church building, and it was torn down. The congregation met in a tent for a year. Again, money was hard to come by. Only with a series of small loans mortgaging the property to the Home Mission Society and a generous donation from Rochester Ford's mother were they finally able to erect a new building at Stone and Council.

Tragedies continued to befall the church; two pastors died while serving. But God had a plan. The revival that had begun in Wales in 1904 spread throughout the world and eventually affected Tucson's church life. Between 1905 and 1907, the membership of First Baptist almost doubled.

New lay leaders came as well. Among them were A. Hazeltine, chairman of the deacons for many years; Dr and Mrs. Thomas; and Judge Fred Fickett.

But even more important was what happened in missions. In 1907 O. E. Comstock, a bivocational preacher and printer, moved to town because of a daughter's tuberculosis. Soon Comstock felt burdened for Tucson's large tubercular community. Once again, personal suffering led to ministry to others (see chapter 7 for more on Comstock).

Comstock bought a house on Adams Street, in the heart of the tubercular community. And there he started a mission under the sponsorship of First Baptist Church. First he organized a Sunday School. Then he added worship services, then a feeding program, and finally a hospital.

The hospital was first called Mercy Hospital, then Comstock Hospital. Finally a hospital building was erected with donations of money and labor. That building still stands, housing the University of Arizona School of Allied Health Sciences.

By 1912, First Baptist Church had two more missions: the Spanish Baptist Mission on South Stone Avenue, which still exists, and the Chinese Baptist Mission, led by Marie Norgaard and Lee Park Lin.

We can get an idea of First Baptist's commitment to missions from its 1910-11 expenditures. The church had $1,894 in expenses and gave $548 for missions. That was more than 20 percent of its income, a double tithe.

Year after year, a handful of people kept First Baptist alive and ministering. Most of them were poor or sick, or both. But they persisted. They were faithful to God's calling and to Christ's Great Commission.

Their faithfulness was to pay off beyond their wildest dreams. On February 24, 1918, Richard Sidney Beal became First Baptist's thirteenth pastor—and stayed for fifty-one years. Things soon began to happen, and kept on happening.

When Dr. Beal came, the church had 203 members. By 1926 there were 1,000, by 1960 around 3,000. Through the years over 200 people from First Baptist went into full-time Christian service. This is a record that has not, to my knowledge, been equaled by any other Tucson Church.

The current site and building date from the mid-1920s.

THE TESTIMONY OF FIRST BAPTIST CHURCH

What does the early history of First Baptist Church say to us today? Let's look at a book of the Bible that means more to me the longer I live—the Book of Job. In chapters 1 and 2 we see the controversy between God and Satan and the trials Job endured as a result. In chapters 3-37 we see the long go-round between Job, his friends, and Elihu. Job's friends are all very earnest and persistent, but they obviously don't know what they're talking about.

In chapters 38-41, God speaks. He always has the last word, doesn't He? What He tells Job, in effect, is this: Job, I am the Creator and Sustainer; you are not. I know what it's all about and where it's all headed; you do not. You've had your say; it's gotten you nowhere. Now trust Me, obey Me, and follow Me.

In verses 2-6 of chapter 42, Job confesses, repents, and submits to God. Then in verse 8, God gives Job an assignment: to pray for his friends. What did that have to do with Job's problem? In God's eyes, it had everything to do with it! Look at verse 10: "After Job had prayed for his friends, the Lord made him prosperous again and gave him twice as much as he had before."

God directed; Job obeyed and prayed; God acted. He acted both on the matter of the friends and on Job's problem. He won the controversy with Satan, straightened out Job's friends, provided for Job, and taught gave many generations a valuable lesson about His ways. But He chose to hinge it all on Job's obedience and prayer. He could have done it some other way. But He chose to prepare and use a human instrument.

So how does this story relate to the history of First Baptist Church? Year after year, a handful of people obeyed Christ by proclaiming His Gospel and obeying His Great Commission. And God honored their prayers and faithfulness.

WHERE IS FIRST BAPTIST CHURCH TODAY?

So here we are at the beginning of the twenty-first century. Where is First Baptist Church today? Right where it was at the beginning of the twentieth century, fighting for its life.

I think the congregation of First Baptist pretty well understands that it is fighting for its life—and that many observers have written it off. Unless God gives First Baptist Church of Tucson a future, it may well have no future to speak of.

But God gave First Baptist a future a century ago. Our forefathers prayed and obeyed, and God honored their prayers and obedience. Will He do less for us?

I believe that First Baptist Church is not only a church of history, but a church of destiny. It is the only one of Tucson's early Protestant churches that still meets in the area where it started. The rest have long since moved to other parts of town. Is this a coincidence? I don't think so. I think it is in accord with the plan and will of God. God has given up neither on that church nor on that part of Tucson.

In the words of Dr. Powell, "This church was planted and sustained by and for our Lord Jesus Christ. It is His face we will now seek."

NOTES TO CHAPTER 10

[1] Abbreviations used in these notes are as follows:
SC Special Collections, Main Library, University of Arizona, Tucson, Arizona.
Dick Hall, "Ointment of Love: Oliver E. Comstock and Tucson's Tent City, Journal of Arizona History (Summer 1976), pp. 111-29, SC.

[2] More information on Comstock is available in SC.

[3] An indication of how the economics of medical care has changed is that in 1931, the hospital's total budget was $12,000.

Further information on TB in Tucson can be found in the Arizona Historical Society Library and the Comstock Foundation, both located in Tucson, in addition to Special Collections.